Logan & The Lonesome Moose

Text and Illustrations Copyright ©
2016 By Stacy Einfalt

I would like to dedicate this story to my little buddy, Logan Tocheny, who continually works hard with his speech therapists to overcome his battle with speech delay.

It was late at night and inside the Lewis family house poor little Logan could not fall asleep. He tries everything, but keeps tossing and turning all night. Finally he gives up and lays on his back staring up at the ceiling. He could feel his tummy tying up in knots just thinking about tomorrow being Monday and how he had to go back to school.

1

Even worse, this week it was his turn to bring something in for show and tell and talk about it in front of his class. Just the thought of it made him cringe. Logan struggles with speech delay, which makes it hard for him to sound out some letters and pronounce his words clearly.

He doesn't have any friends at school. The other kids make fun of and tease him about how he talks. It makes him feel sad.

No sooner did he drift off to sleep he could hear his alarm clock sounding off. He pulled the covers up over his head and let out a groan, not looking forward to facing another day of being picked on at school. Suddenly he could hear his Mom calling out to him from down in the kitchen, "Logan, come on, time to get up! I'm making blueberry pancakes!"

Logan left out another groan as he crawled out of bed, yawned and stretched. A smile came across his face as he could smell the aroma of blueberry pancakes in the air. He quickly got dressed and ran downstairs to the kitchen

He sat down at the table where a stack of warm blueberry pancakes was waiting for him. He drizzled some yummy maple syrup over the stack before gobbling them down.

When he finished he rested his chin in his hands as he stared down at the empty plate, trying to figure out what he could take in for show and tell later that week. His Mom could see that something was bothering him and asked, "What's wrong sweetheart?"

Logan mumbled to his Mom in his jumbled talk, "I still haven't figured out what I'm going to take in for show and tell this Friday." His Mom smiled and said, "Don't worry. You'll figure something out."

Logan got up from the table, grabbed his backpack and headed towards the front door. His Mom called out to him, "Have a great day!" Logan just left out another groan in response as he headed out the door.

No sooner did he start on his walk to school he ran into Matthew, Marcus, and Micah, who too were heading the same way. The boys followed behind Logan and immediately began picking on him about how he speaks. Logan just stared down at his feet as he continued to walk along trying to ignore the laughter and teasing from the other kids.

Logan was feeling sad. He wished others would look past the way he spoke and try to get to know him. They'd see that he is a lot like them. He just wanted to be accepted. The school day seemed to be dragging by as Logan was feeling alone and isolated from the other kids. He was last to be picked when choosing teams to play kickball during recess.

At lunch time he sat and ate all by himself at a table in the corner of the cafeteria while watching his classmates sitting together at the other tables, laughing and giggling, while enjoying their lunches.

Finally, even though it felt like forever, the last bell of the day rang for school dismissal. Logan grabbed his backpack and headed out of the school. He began making his way back home, again having to deal with the laughter and teasing from the other kids.

When he arrived home his Mom was waiting for him in the kitchen with his favorite snack of sliced apples smeared with peanut butter. "How was your day?" she asked. Logan replied with a groan as he sunk his teeth into a slice of apple. With his jumbled talk Logan asked his Mom if he could take his snack and go down to the stream behind their house to skip rocks across the water. Knowing that, that always cheers him up his Mom said, "Sure honey, go ahead."

While walking back to the stream, Logan began trying to think of something he could take in for show and tell. He was growing anxious having only a few days left and still not able to come up with an idea.

As he arrived at the bank by the stream he saw a lonesome baby moose wading in the water getting a drink. Logan and the moose stared at one another with their eyes both wide open in excitement.

Logan shouted out in his jumbled talk, "Wow! Where did you come from?" The young moose turned around to run off when Logan quieted his voice and said, "I'm sorry. I didn't mean to scare you. Please don't go." The moose stopped in his tracks, turned back and looked over at him.

Logan slowly took small steps getting closer as he reached his hand that was holding a slice of apple out, offering it to the moose. The moose, still nervous, stretched out his neck to sniff at the apple. Logan spoke softly reassuring him by saying, "Don't worry. I promise I won't hurt you." The moose gently took the apple from his hand with his lips and began munching on it. Logan smiled as he realized that the moose didn't seem to mind how he spoke.

When finished the moose climbed up onto the bank to join Logan as he held out his hand offering him another slice of apple in which he kindly accepted. As he was enjoying the last slice Logan asked, "Will you be my friend?" The moose reached down and gently nuzzled his face. Logan happily exclaimed, "I guess that means yes!" He thought for a moment and said, "I think I will call you Manny."

19

Suddenly an idea popped into Logan's head. He finally figured out what he wanted to take in for show and tell! He was going to take his new best friend, Manny the moose! He was so excited. He couldn't wait to get home to tell his parents. He motioned his hand and said, "Come Manny, let's go home!"

Manny followed Logan along the path that led back to his house. When they reached his backyard, Logan turned to Manny, raised his hand and said, "Stay." Manny stood and watched as Logan turned and ran into the house.

Once inside he burst into the kitchen where his Mom was preparing dinner while his Dad was setting the table. "Guess what!" Logan exclaimed, "I decided what I'm going to take for show and tell!"

His parents glanced at one another with a smile. His Dad asked,"So what have you decided to take?" Logan said, "Come outside and I will show you." As his parents followed him out the door their mouths dropped open as they let out a big gasp when they saw the baby moose standing in their backyard.

Logan motioned for him to come over to them. Manny lowered his head as Logan reached up to pet him, while his parents watched on with concern, but were amazed at how gentle and well connected the young moose was with their son. "Where did he come from?" his Dad asked. "I found him down by the stream," Logan replied. "I named him Manny. Can we keep him, PLEASE?"

Although still having some concern, his parents agreed that Manny could stay in their back yard for as long as he wished. Logan shouted, "Yippee! Did you hear that Manny? Welcome to your new home," as he gave Manny a big hug.

Logan and his parents headed inside to have dinner leaving Manny in the backyard. After dinner, Logan finished his homework and gave his Mom and Dad a kiss good night before heading upstairs to get ready for bed.

He brushed his teeth, got dressed in his pj's and headed over to his bedroom window. As he gazed out he saw Manny curled up, nestled in the backyard, snoozing soundly underneath the starlit sky. Logan whispered softly, "Good night Manny."

He then headed over, climbed into his bed, closed his eyes and began dreaming about his new best friend.

Morning arrived and Logan was up and out of bed before his alarm even had a chance to wake him. He quickly got dressed and rushed downstairs towards the kitchen where his Mom was making him breakfast. As he ran past her she said, "Whoa! What's the rush? What about breakfast?" Logan shouted, "I have to say good morning to Manny first."

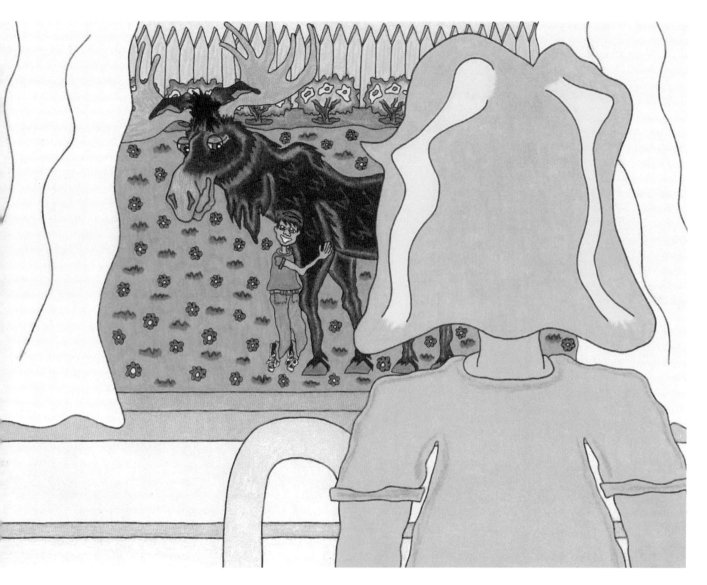

Forgetting all about their visitor, Logan's Mom looked out the kitchen window in disbelief as she saw the young moose still in their backyard accepting a big hug from her son. "Good morning Manny," Logan said as he hugged him tight. "Now don't worry, I have to go to school, but I will be back. You promise to be here, right?" Logan asked. Manny slowly lowered his head looking into Logan's eyes, as if letting him know he understood.

Logan said good bye to Manny before heading back into the house where he gobbled down the yummy breakfast his Mom made for him. Once finished he grabbed his backpack and yelled, "See ya Mom!" as he headed out the front door and off to school.

Logan was feeling like school didn't seem so bad today, even though some of the other kids were still picking on him for how he spoke. He didn't pay any attention to their teasing. He just kept thinking about how he couldn't wait to get home to see his new friend Manny.

Before he knew it the school day was over and Logan was leaving, heading home. The closer he got to home the faster he ran until he reached his back yard where he found Manny waiting for him.

He looked just as happy to see Logan as he started walking over towards him. "Hi Manny!" Logan exclaimed, "How was your day? I missed you!" Manny lowered his head and blew a warm breath out of his nose onto Logan's face letting him know that he missed him too.

The next few days went by so fast.

Each day Logan would rush home from school to find Manny waiting for him. He was excited and ready to practice the different tricks Logan was teaching him to perform for show and tell.

It's now Friday morning, Logan was feeling nervous and uneasy just thinking about standing and having to speak in front of his classmates. "What if I can't make my words come out correctly when I speak? What if they make fun of me again? What if they don't like Manny?" These were some of the questions that kept haunting him as he, his Mom, Dad and Manny were walking along, heading to his school.

37

When they arrived at his school Logan's teacher and classmates were standing out front waiting for them. As they approached them their eyes grew wide. Some of them looked scared, some excited. Logan took in a big breath and glanced up at Manny, who lowered his head, reassuring Logan he was there for him. Logan took in another breath then said, "Hi. This is my friend Manny. He is a moose. Would you like to see him do some tricks I've taught him?" A few of the children excitedly shouted out, "Yes!" as Logan asked Manny to "sit".

Logan's classmates were amazed as they watched on. They were so impressed with how well Manny listened to Logan that they didn't even take notice to his jumbled talk. They realized he was pretty cool and felt bad that they hadn't taken a chance to get to know him better because of how he spoke.

39

Matthew, one of the boys that teased Logan raised his hand and said, "Logan, we're sorry for teasing you. Will you and Manny be our friends?" A smile beamed across Logan's face as he finally felt accepted. He enthusiastically replied, "Yes!" as the other kids began to cheer and gather around Manny and him.

Made in the USA
Middletown, DE
26 January 2024

48621568R00027